# Heart of Beginnings

## A Sweet Southern Island Romance - Prequel Novella

## Jenny Fawn

**Happily Ever Always Publications**

Published by Happily Ever Always Publications

ISBN: 979-8-9858945-0-9 (paperback)

Cover Art: Pixabay.com

Printed by KDP

JennyFawnBooks.com

Formatted with Atticus

# Table of Contents

❤

*J - You can, and you will.*

## Chapter 1

♥

## John - 35 Years Ago

THE CHOPPY WAVES OF the Atlantic Ocean battered the bow of my small aluminum boat. Thankfully, the waves were much calmer than they were just twenty four hours prior, when Hurricane Louisa pounded the coast of South Carolina, because this boat wasn't really intended for ocean use.

The category one hurricane certainly hadn't been the most significant storm to make landfall along our shores, but the damage was still widespread and substantial.

As usual, my father only had one thing in mind with the storm's destruction: how could he profit from it?

I shook my head in disgust as I zipped through the waves. My father owned Franklin Builders, a very successful construction company that he had started himself when he wasn't much older than my twenty two years. But his success had come at a steep price. He had sold his soul a long, long time ago when it came to ethical business practices. Gouging people in their time of need was his bread and butter nowadays.

Good old dad was a slick businessman, but I didn't understand how the decent people of coastal South Carolina hadn't figured him out yet. I had firsthand knowledge that he used sub-par materials and often hired cheap, unqualified workers. Yet, after all these years, he was able to convince people that his company was trustworthy.

When I showed up for work this morning, ready to do whatever I could to help with the storm damage, he informed me I would be in charge of 'recon.' That was his code for letting me know he wanted me to go out among the victims of the storm and figure out where he could make the most money. In other words, my job was to find out which businesses or homeowners would pay a premium price for his company's 'premium' services.

Well, I was done with his games. I quit my job, right there on the spot. I told him I would no longer be a part of his unethical business practices, and that I would rather give up my job than take advantage of one more person during their time of need.

Of course, he slapped back at me in his typical fashion. I was too soft. *Blah*. I believed I was better than him. *Blah, blah*. I had no idea what it took to make it in this business. *Blah, blah, blah*. I had heard it a million times before.

When I told him again that I was done with him, he threw my tool bag down at my feet and told me to get out and not come back.

So I did.

We never had the best of relationships, so his reaction didn't surprise me in the least. But now that I finally stood up to him, well, I'm pretty sure he didn't see that coming. Yeah, maybe it took me twenty two years, and I probably should have done it sooner, but now it was done. And I would never go back.

As I drove away, I wondered how I could use my skills as a carpenter and general handyman to actually *help* people affected by the storm. I thought about all the resorts and tourist towns along the South Carolina coast where I lived. Sure, there was damage. But there were many construction companies nearby that could help these people. I wanted to think outside the box.

Then suddenly, a memory popped into my head about an island a few miles off the coast where some friends and I had gone on a whim the previous summer to play a round of golf. I wasn't much of a golfer, but I went anyway. I was glad that I did.

It wasn't a tourist trap or a haven of wealthy beach homes. It was a small island with a town full of hardworking, normal folks just like me. I had fallen in love with it the moment I set foot on the island, but I hadn't been back since.

But that was going to change today.

It was a place where I knew the big construction companies, whose only interest was to make money, would ignore during a crisis like this. But like a lot of places around here, I was sure there was damage, and I was sure they would need help.

And I was going to give it to them.

I went home to the house I lived in with my dad, and threw everything that mattered to me in a duffle bag. Besides some clothes and my tools, I didn't have much, so it didn't take long. When I finished, I drove to my friend Jeremy Marshall's house and picked up my boat. I stored her on a trailer in his backyard because my dad didn't know I owned her, so there was no way I could have kept her at our house. Then I headed to the nearest marina with a functional launch.

And now, as I raised my hand to shield my eyes from the glare of the sun on the waves of the Atlantic, Heartsail Island came into view. I knew I made the right decision.

*Chapter 2*

♥

## Nora

OKAY. SO MAYBE BETH had been right. I probably shouldn't have stayed down here last night when the storm came ashore. And I definitely shouldn't have done it alone. There had been moments when I thought it was all going to come crashing down on top of me.

But there was no way I was going to leave this place now that it was mine. I was Nora Weatherly, gosh darn it, and The Heartsail Inn was my responsibility.

Plus, it was all that I had left of my grandfather.

It had been me and Gramps against the world for over half my life. When my dad died in a military training exercise when I was a baby, momma and I had come here to live with Gramps. But when she passed away from ovarian cancer when I was ten, Gramps was the only family I had left.

The lovely inn and golf course used to be Heartsail Island's most popular destination. The property, which spanned the entire southern portion of Heartsail Island, once boasted ten deluxe guest rooms in the main house and five quaint beach cabins. We would be booked solid - year-round - with guests who came to enjoy more than a thousand beautiful acres of golf course, beaches, dunes, and walking trails. To me, it was simply home.

But the last few years had been a struggle. Gramps had contracted a virus several years ago that weakened the muscles of his heart, and he could not handle the upkeep of the inn and cabins. I did as much as I could, but I was barely out of high school and taking care of Gramps had been a full-time job. As the medical bills piled up, necessary repairs often got passed over, which meant that, after a while, the main inn and cabins were no longer suitable for guests.

But now he was gone too. Just over six months ago, Gramps passed peacefully in his sleep. And at twenty one years old, I was truly alone.

Thankfully, the golf course still brought in a steady stream of income to keep me afloat, but my home was nothing like it used to be.

I had worked really hard over the last six months to bring the inn back to its former glory. After I paid his medical bills, I used the rest of Gramps's life insurance to do most of the repairs to the main house that were required before I could start having guests again.

I had gotten *so* close. In fact, I even had scheduled a soft open with some island residents and friends in just a few weeks.

But then Hurricane Louisa hit.

Now, as I surveyed the damage from the outside of the inn, my heart was breaking all over again.

Large sections of shingles were missing from the roof. Three sets of storm shutters failed, which led to broken windows and interior water damage in some of the guest rooms. And the worst part, the deck that spanned the entire back of the inn overlooking the beach, had been torn off and destroyed.

Thankfully, the house was built to withstand storms much more powerful than Louisa, so structurally the building was sound.

But I had spent all of my money on the repairs that had just been completed. I didn't know how I would come back from this.

But like I said, I was Nora Weatherly, and this was my home. As I climbed inside Gramps's beat up old pickup truck to make my way into town, I vowed I would bring this place back to its former glory.

Again.

I had no other option.

*Chapter 3*

♥

# John

THE DOCK AT THE marina looked sturdy and intact as I came ashore on Heartsail Island. I was glad to see that the western side of the island hadn't sustained too much damage. It probably wasn't unusual, as it took less of a direct hit than the eastern side would have. But, besides a significant mess of tree limbs and other storm debris, the damage seemed minimal.

Many folks were out and about, surveying the area around the marina and cleaning up debris on the shoreline. I pulled into an empty slip and tied my boat to the dock before grabbing my bags and hopping out. I slung my duffle over my head and across my chest, making it easier to carry.

As I made my way up the dock, an older man emerged from a small blue building with a sign indicating that it was the marina office. "Good morning, son. Can I help you?" he asked with a tired look on his tanned face. His gray hair was covered with a battered cap that said *Heartsail Marina* in faded blue embroidery.

"Hello, sir," I said, removing my sunglasses and reaching out my hand in a proper greeting. "My name is John Franklin. I live on the mainland. I have a construction background, so I thought I'd come over and see if I could help y'all out with any repairs here on the island. Louisa packed quite a wallop last night."

The old man's wrinkled face split into a wide smile. "Well, that's mighty kind of you, John," he replied. "Name's Mick Hunter. I own this marina. We don't often get much help from the mainland. We usually do a fair job of fending for ourselves here on Heartsail. But you're right," he agreed with a frown. "Miss Louisa sure had a bee in her bonnet last evening. Made a right mess of our pretty little island." He gestured toward the debris that littered the shoreline and the area surrounding the marina.

"I've got myself a good supply of staff and volunteers to help get the marina and ferry service back into shape. Thankfully, we didn't sustain any significant damage here, just one heck of a mess," he said. "But if you ventured into town a ways, I'm sure you will come across someone who could use your help. You're welcome to leave your boat here. Won't even charge you a slip fee, seeing as you're here to help."

I smiled at the old man and shook his hand again. "Much obliged, Mick," I said, thankful to have a safe place to dock. She may not look like much, but I loved that little boat. I'd purchased her when I was just sixteen from an older gentleman in our neighborhood. He'd offered me a great deal in exchange for helping him out with some free repairs (unbeknownst to my father, of course). At the time, I hadn't even owned a vehicle to tow her with, but she was the first thing I could call my own.

I had just assumed that I would have to pull her up on a beach somewhere and hope for the best. Island hospitality at its finest came to the rescue, however, as I waved to Mick and headed down the road toward town. This was already turning out to be a MUCH better plan than helping my father swindle people in need.

*Chapter 4*

♥

## Nora

THE MID-AUGUST HEAT AND humidity soaked through my bright yellow tank top, making my skin feel sticky and gross. Usually the southern summer heat didn't bother me. I couldn't imagine spending my life anywhere that the sun didn't shine ninety percent of the year.

But today, it was making me cranky. I was sure it had more to do with the situation I currently found myself in, rather than the heat itself. But I wasn't in the mood to analyze myself. I had stuff to do. I just didn't quite know how to go about doing it.

The trip to the hardware store had nearly emptied my personal bank account. I currently had $38 in my wallet, which had to last me until the golf course was up and running again. Thank goodness the inn's business account had enough to continue to pay Harry, the long-time manager of the golf course, for several weeks. At least I wouldn't have to lay him off. That was, IF we could get the course opened in the next few days.

Several sheets of drywall, multiple bundles of shingles, three new windows, and lumber for new hurricane shutters were piled high in the truck's bed. Thankfully, Sam, the owner of the store, had let me open a tab to cover the cost of the replacement windows.

As for the deck? Well, that would just have to wait.

I sat at a table in the shade of an umbrella outside the cafe in town. I needed to figure out what my next steps should be. The cafe was closed for some minor repairs, but my best friend Beth Dobson was the daughter of the owners, so she brought me a tall glass of sweet tea as I planned out my next move.

"Thank you so much," I said as I pulled my long, light brown ponytail away from my sweaty neck and placed the cool glass against my skin. "Are you sure there's nothing I can do to help y'all clean up?" I asked. Beth and I had been best friends since kindergarten, and she and her parents had been like family since my mom passed when I was ten.

Now that Gramps was gone, too, they were all I had left.

"Nah," she replied with a wave. "There's no serious damage at all. Just a little water around the doors that left a bit of a mess inside. We should be good to open within the hour."

She plopped down on the chair across from me and fanned herself. "Golly, it's humid today," she complained. Her long blonde hair was piled high on her head, and her porcelain skin was tinged with pink. "I'm glad we didn't lose power so we can at least run some fans inside the cafe and have service up and running by lunchtime. Daddy said they didn't know how long it would take for all the power to be restored to the rest of the island, so A/C is off the table for the time being."

Besides being the owner of the cafe, Beth's father was also the mayor of Heartsail Island. He was off surveying the rest of the island and had checked in with her mom a few hours ago with a status update. Luckily, we hadn't heard of any serious damage or injuries. Lots of debris and uprooted trees, yes. Major structural damages and loss of life, thank the Lord, no.

It was true. The storm had not affected power in the town proper of Heartsail Island. But unfortunately, down on my lonely southern tip, it would probably be awhile until they could restore it.

"Nora, are you sure you don't want to stay with us until you get things repaired at the inn?" she asked, a familiar look of concern passing over her pretty face. I loved Beth. She was my best friend in the entire world. But the thought of leaving the inn while it was in disrepair just didn't sit well with me.

"Nah," I replied. "I'll be fine. I'm going to put plastic over the broken windows until I can find someone to help me install the new ones. But most of the other work I can do myself. It's my responsibility now." I knew Beth could hear the resolve in my voice by the look on her face. She knew me well enough to know that my stubbornness would win out over any arguments she tried to make, so she didn't bother trying.

"Ok," she said, rising to head back inside the cafe. "Just make sure you stop by before heading home and we'll have a cooler of food ready for you to take with you. Don't bother arguing," she said as I opened my mouth to protest, and she walked toward the door. "Momma already started putting it together. She'll just bring it down herself if you don't stop and pick it up."

As she left, I sighed and waved. I hated it when people felt sorry for me. I knew that Beth's mom, Miss Daisy, loved me like a daughter, and that she would do the same for Beth, but it still made me feel uncomfortable.

But I couldn't worry about that right now. I had to come up with a way to find someone to help with the repairs, even though I had no money to pay them.

*Chapter 5*

♥

# John

I ADJUSTED THE STRAP of my duffle bag on my shoulder and shifted my tool bag to the opposite hand as I approached the center of town. It wasn't an overly long walk from the marina, but the humidity was high and I could feel a patch of sweat forming on the back of my t-shirt. I was glad I changed into shorts before I left the mainland. The idea of denim covering my long legs made me sweat just thinking about it.

Looking around, there seemed to be a real sense of community here on the island. As I walked down the residential street toward the middle of town, I saw neighbors helping neighbors clean up debris, downed tree limbs, and palmetto fronds. Sand bags, most likely used for flood protection, sat in neat stacks on the sidewalks outside of houses and storefronts.

Turning off the road from the marina, I made my way down the sidewalk of Main Street. Live oaks, draped with hanging Spanish moss, and palmetto trees dotted the open grassy area across the street. I imagined it was a beautiful little town square when not covered in hurricane mess.

Since I wasn't familiar with the island, I wasn't sure where to begin. I spotted a small cafe that appeared to be open for business and figured I might as well start there.

A young woman sat hunched in the shade of an umbrella at one of the small outdoor tables with a glass of sweet tea. Strands of light brown hair that had escaped from her ponytail partially hid her face. She appeared to be writing something and didn't glance in my direction, so I approached the table to see if she could help me.

"Ahem. Excuse me, Miss," I said, clearing my throat to get her attention. She raised her head and pushed her hair back, revealing piercing blue eyes and the most beautiful face I had ever seen. Her bowed lips turned upward in a slight smile, and her pretty face was flushed a light pink from the heat. I stared, mute for a moment, as what felt like a jolt of electricity zapped my entire body.

"Can I help you?" she asked with a raised eyebrow, when I continued to stand there staring at her, like some kind of crazy lunatic. Her light southern drawl flowed over me like warm maple syrup. I shook the cobwebs out of my scrambled brain and attempted to speak.

"Oh. Right. Sorry," I stuttered. Goodness, I sounded like a moron! I cleared my throat and tried again. "Hi. I was wondering if you could help me with something," I said, glad that I could form a coherent sentence. "I just came over from the mainland to help with storm damage. Since I don't actually know anyone here on the island, I was wondering if you could point me toward someone who might need a handyman. I have construction experience, so I wanted to offer my services."

Her eyes grew wide as I spoke, and I wondered if I offended her. "I'm sorry," I said quickly, raising my hand in apology. "I didn't mean to assume y'all couldn't fend for yourselves..."

"No, no!" she said with a quick shake of her head. "I'm sorry! You caught me off guard." She let out a small laugh and slid the paper she had been writing on across the table in my direction. "Actually, I'm looking for help with some repairs myself. I was just going to post this outside the grocery store."

The hand written sign read:

*URGENT HELP NEEDED*
*AT HEARTSAIL INN*
*WILL PAY IN FREE GOLF*
*CALL NORA*

"Free golf?" I asked as I picked up the sign to examine it. Well, that wouldn't really do much to help me find a place to stay here on the island.

She looked down at the table. "Funds are a little short at the moment," she said, running her finger down the side of her glass. "I was hoping I could find someone willing to barter." She shrugged her slim shoulders, looking embarrassed.

Suddenly, a brilliant idea popped into my mind. It was like fate chose this moment to hand over the solution to my most pressing need on a silver platter. "Heartsail Inn, huh? Well, Nora... I'm assuming you are Nora, right?" I asked, and she nodded in confirmation. "Golf is fun and all, but I have a better idea. How about we work out a different sort of deal?"

I threw one of my famous half-smiles her way, hoping that she would go along with my plan.

*Chapter 6*

♥

## Nora

I RAISED MY EYEBROW at him, wondering what the young stranger had in mind. His cocky half-smile, while incredibly appealing, made me think that this ridiculously handsome man could be trouble. "May I?" he asked, gesturing at the chair across from me at the small cafe table.

"Sure, why not?" I replied. I pushed the chair out with my foot under the small table, trying to seem nonchalant. A different sort of deal? I didn't know what this guy had in mind, but my curiosity and desperation for help outweighed my skepticism at this point.

When he lifted his duffle bag over his head and off his shoulder, I could see the ripple of well-toned muscles in his arm and chest. The hem of his t-shirt rose slightly, revealing just a peek of his tanned and toned torso. Wowza. A wave of heat rose inside my body, but it had nothing to do with the temperature outside.

I wasn't typically a girl who drooled over men. That was more Beth's style. I dated a bit in high school, but my life was too busy for that kind of distraction these days. Sure, I'd seen my fill of handsome, business-type guys come through the golf course over the years, but none of them had ever really interested me. I'd been young, of course - barely out of high school - when we were still taking guests at the inn, so I never interacted with them closely. But even now that I was twenty one, I still didn't feel a pull toward that type of guy. Buttoned up and clean cut? No thanks. Too stuffy for my taste.

But I definitely appreciated what I was seeing in front of me right now. My surprise visitor sat down at the shaded table and removed his dark sunglasses. His chocolate brown eyes gazed at me as he continued to flash the half-smile. His dark, wind-blown hair had light streaks from the sun. My sudden urge to run my fingers through it, just to see if it was as soft as it looked, took me by surprise.

"John Franklin," he said. He reached over the table to introduce himself. A lightning bolt of electricity pulsed up my arm when he enveloped my smaller hand inside his. His palm, calloused and rough, caused a ripple of excitement in me. This was the hand of a man who worked for a living. Not a pampered businessman who spent his days schmoozing on a golf course.

I blinked rapidly as I pulled my hand out of his grasp. Trying desperately to control my raging hormones, I cleared my throat. "Nora Weatherly," I replied, embarrassed that my voice sounded slightly breathy.

"Pleasure to meet you, Nora," he said with another sexy smile as he leaned forward and rested his arms on the small tabletop between us. "So, tell me about your project at the inn. Are you an employee there?"

I sat up straight in my chair and lifted my chin defiantly. "As a matter of fact, I'm the *owner* of Heartsail Inn and Golf Course," I said with an edge. This wasn't the first time someone who didn't know my situation had mistaken me for a staff member. I knew it was unusual for someone my age to own a business like that, but I still bristled when they made that type of assumption.

Most people laughed, or didn't believe me when I told them I owned such a well-established business. But his reaction wasn't at all like that. He leaned back in his chair and crossed his arms over his chest. "The owner, huh? Nice," he said with an admiring nod. "That's impressive, Nora."

My mouth dropped open slightly. His easy acceptance of my position surprised me. "Um, thanks," I replied awkwardly.

"So, the project?" he prompted again. "What exactly is it you need help with?"

"Right," I said, adopting a more professional tone. "Well, the inn sustained some damage during the storm last night. A few broken storm shutters and windows, some missing shingles, things like that." I decided to forgo telling him about the deck, since I couldn't afford the materials it would require to fix it right now, anyway. "Do you think that would be something you could help with?"

He nodded slowly. "Yeah, Nora," he said with another one of those smiles. "I think I could help. But, here's my idea. I don't have anywhere to stay here on the island, and money is kinda tight at the moment. So, I thought, instead of payment or free golf," he said, gesturing at the sign I had made, "how about you hook me up with room and board at the inn in exchange for my labor?"

I narrowed my eyes at him as I mulled over his suggestion. Room and board? Like, as in, he would live with me for the foreseeable future?

Hmm... I guess I would need to get used to people staying at the inn once I was up and running again, but I'd never had guests when it was just me running the place. When Gramps was alive, we'd had additional staff members on site at all times. Plus, of course, Gramps was there.

But now, it was just me. Alone. We'd had to let the staff go when Gramps's health had deteriorated and we closed for guests. Was I ready to let a stranger into my home, with no one else around for miles? Especially a stranger who looked like John Franklin? I had to admit the idea made me nervous. But if I was going to make the inn a success, I needed to get comfortable with the idea, STAT.

"Nora?" he prompted, as my silence stretched on. "What do you think? Free labor in exchange for room and board?"

I looked at John for a few seconds longer. Yes, he was handsome as sin, and I didn't know him from Adam. But I was desperate. I needed help, and it seemed that God had plopped him down right in my path. I could totally handle this.

"Deal." I said and stuck out my hand to shake on it.

Chapter 7

♥

# John

I COULDN'T BELIEVE MY luck. I wasn't an overly religious man, because my father had never taken me to church as a child. But as I cruised down the road in a beat up old pickup truck with a beautiful woman behind the wheel, I sent up a quick prayer of thanks to whoever handed down this small miracle.

Not only had my abrupt state of unemployment lasted less than three hours, but I was also going to be living in the same place as this beautiful, blue eyed stranger for the foreseeable future.

She'd been quiet since we climbed into her heavily loaded truck and set off toward Heartsail Inn. I could practically feel the tension radiating off her in waves. I knew this must be a weird situation for her, so I decided I should do my best to ease some of the tension.

"So, Nora," I said, "tell me about yourself. How did you find yourself the owner of an inn and golf course at such a young age? You can't be much older than twenty."

"I'm twenty one," she said, as she tucked her blowing hair behind her ear. She stuck her hand out the open window and waved at a man near the clubhouse of the golf course I had played at last summer. I remembered him. He had been a jovial fellow who took wonderful care of my friends and me when we were here, despite being quite busy. I didn't remember seeing any other employees, which, now that I think about it, struck me as rather odd for a business like that.

We continued further down the road, the golf course on one side and a maritime forest on the other, before she spoke again. "I inherited this place from my grandfather when he passed away several months ago. I've lived here almost my whole life. Now it's mine." She peered through the windshield with sadness on her beautiful face.

"I'm so sorry for your loss, Nora." I knew what it was like to lose someone you loved. When my mother left when I was six, my grandmother moved in with dad and me. She was my rock when I was younger, and I'm pretty sure she's the only reason I had any morals or manners at all. Gran had loved me fiercely, and the feeling was completely mutual. But the summer after my fifteenth birthday, she suffered a massive stroke and passed away with no warning. The pain of the loss had nearly crippled me.

Though he had always played fast and loose with the rules in his business, that was when my dad really started ramping up his con game. Life had never been the same for me after I lost my Gran. When she died, I knew deep down there was no way dad would ever go back to being an honorable businessman, but I also knew that I had no intention of turning out like him.

"Here we are," Nora said as we pulled up in front of the beautiful old inn. The large, three story structure stood tall and proud in front of the dunes at the southern tip of Heartsail Island. Two magnolia trees flanked a stone walkway that led from the circular drive to the wide front porch that spanned the entire front of the inn. Thick bunches of wax myrtle, azalea, and saw palmetto shrubs dotted the pine straw-covered gardens along the length of the pretty porch. While it was empty now, I imagined it was usually filled with porch swings, rocking chairs, and other comfortable furniture.

While the inn's pretty white hanging sign had partially come loose from its post, the white siding looked to have weathered the storm well. Most of the palmetto and other trees I could see along the edge of the dunes behind the building seemed to be in good shape as well. The inn was lovely, and I could see why Nora held such a fondness in her heart for it.

From the front of the building, I could see some of the damage she had mentioned. There was a large patch of shingles missing on the front slope of the roof, near one of the broken shutters on a third story window. The damage didn't look too bad at first glance, but in my line of work, I knew looks could be deceiving. Water had a way of making everything more complicated, and we had a ton of it last night, thanks to good old Hurricane Louisa.

"So, I guess I can start by showing you around outside so you can see what needs fixing. Then we can unload the truck and get to work." Nora climbed out of the truck and pointed up toward the broken window. "That is one of the broken windows. There's some water damage inside that guest room, as well as two other third floor rooms around the back of the inn. You can see that patch of missing shingles there." She pointed toward the roof. "I didn't notice any water damage in the attic when I checked earlier, but you can look, too, to see if you find anything. There are two more broken windows and more shingles off on the back slope of the roof as well. We can take a walk around there so you can see. Just be careful of the mess."

I hadn't yet commented on my perceived scope of the project to Nora, but from first glance, I didn't think this job was going to take more than a few days to complete. I wondered if I made a miscalculation with our deal, because I had a feeling I would need to find another place to hang my hat much sooner than I first thought.

Until we rounded the corner of the back of the inn.

"Oh, man," I said, as I whistled out a breath. A large deck, which looked to have at one time spanned the entire back of the building, was now nothing more than a pile of mangled lumber, railing, and furniture that littered the grassy area between the inn and dunes. "Uh... You neglected to mention the missing deck when we talked about the repairs." I glanced at her, and I could see the sadness in her eyes as she looked at the rubble.

"Yeah." Her voice was thick with emotion. "You don't need to worry about that. Besides helping me clean up the mess, I won't be replacing it."

I looked at her in confusion. "Why wouldn't you want to fix it, Nora?" I looked from the inn out over the beach. "I can't imagine not wanting to have a deck back here for your guests to enjoy. This view is incredible." The tide was out, which meant that the stretch of beach just beyond the wooden walkway through the well-spaced palmetto trees and dunes was quite expansive. The waves curled onto the shore, where gulls called out to one another in search of a good meal. A few yards out over the water, a pelican dove toward the sea to scoop up his lunch.

"It's not that I don't want to replace it, John." She shrugged in what I can only assume was defeat, then her shoulders sagged with sadness. "I can't." She turned away from me as her finger darted up to her lashes to wipe away a stray tear.

It was at that moment that I decided, although I didn't know how I was going to make it happen, I *was* going to give Nora her deck.

## Chapter 8

♥

## Nora

THE DAY PASSED IN a flurry of hammers, nails, and crowbars. Since the power was still out, we had to do everything the old fashioned way. Brute strength with no power tools.

I spent most of the day pulling out wet drywall around the broken windows. It was a messy, miserable job, but the smashing and yanking helped me get out some of my frustration.

The wood floors in the two back guest rooms sustained a bit of water damage, but hopefully the power would come back on soon and I could get some fans running to help dry them quickly. I crossed my fingers that they would dry without too much warping or staining, because, like the deck, there was no way I could afford to replace them.

John focused on replacing the missing shingles for most of the day. He agreed with my assessment in the attic, so thankfully there was no need to replace any of the roof.

Several times throughout the day, I caught myself watching him through the window as he hefted bundles of shingles up to the roof. He worked shirtless, which was probably a safety hazard, but I had absolutely no complaints. He was definitely a fine specimen of a man. His strong shoulders and chest tapered down to a perfect six-pack and narrow waist, and the heat of the day made his tanned body glisten with sweat.

At one point, I watched as he took a break to cool off with a dip in the ocean, and I nearly fell out of the open window as I leaned out to get a better view.

I'm pretty sure he saw me gawking at him at least once, but hopefully, I only imagined the smirk I thought I saw on his handsome face.

I was hot and cranky, so once I got the plastic secured to the final broken window, I decided it was time to call it a day. The sun was just beginning to set, so I felt like I'd put in enough work to be satisfied.

After a quick, cool shower, I headed to the kitchen to raid the huge cooler that Miss Daisy had insisted I bring home with me earlier. The puff of cool air felt like heaven on my face when I opened it.

No wonder the thing had been so heavy I couldn't carry it myself! Miss Daisy had gone way overboard with her generosity. Inside, I found a huge selection of my favorite deli sandwiches, pasta salads, fresh cut fruit, an array of desserts, and a large jug of her fresh brewed sweet tea. There was enough ice surrounding everything that John and I should be well fed for several days, even without electricity.

"Hey Nora?" John called from the front door when he came inside. I hoped he finally decided that it was time to call it a day, too. All the hammering on the roof had given me a dull headache, and I was ready for some quiet.

"In the kitchen," I called out, and a moment later he appeared in the doorway. Lord, this man was beautiful. He stood in the doorway, dirty and sweaty from a hard day of work, but my body still had a swift and uncontrollable reaction to him.

"Hey." He stopped just inside the doorway and eyed the cooler. "I'm done with the roof, and I got the drywall you tossed out on the porch roof cleaned up. Since it is getting dark, I'm calling it a day. Mind if I grab a quick shower before dinner?" We had survived the day on nothing but granola bars and water, so I was certain he must be just as famished as me.

"Of course not. Let me show you to your room." I closed the lid on the cooler. He smirked a bit as I led him down the hallway to the foot of the stairs where he had left his duffle bag earlier in the day. "So formal," he laughed. "I guess it is just second nature for you to use that phrase, having grown up in an inn and all."

I chuckled at his reaction as we climbed the stairs to the second floor. "Yeah, I guess I have said it once or twice over the years." I opened the door to my favorite guest room and led him inside. It was on the western side of the inn, so it currently had a view of the beautiful sunset from the opened windows. The gauzy white curtains fluttered in the breeze. I had decorated the large room with pale blue paint and whitewashed furniture. A beautiful king sized bed, covered in a blue quilt with tiny yellow and white flowers, was the focal point of the room.

"There are five guest rooms on this floor, and five more upstairs. Each room has a private bath and spectacular views." I went through my typical spiel as I opened the door to his bath. He remained quiet as I fluttered around the room, showing him where everything was. When I finished, I made my way over to the window to look at the sky, which was currently glowing orange like fire. "This is my favorite room in the whole inn. It used to be my room, actually. When I was younger, I'd sit by this window almost every night and watch the sunset." I wasn't exactly sure why I told him that, but it just seemed to pop out of my mouth without me even thinking about it.

"Why isn't it your room anymore?" John asked quietly. He had moved next to me to look out the window, and just being near him made my body tingle. I took a step back to put a little distance between us.

With a deep breath, I shook off my nostalgia and flipped back into business mode. It didn't do anyone any good to dwell on the past, especially me. "I moved downstairs into Gramps's room after he died. It made no sense to heat or cool the rooms up here if I didn't need to, so it was just more practical being downstairs in the owner's room."

He nodded as he stepped toward the luggage rack where he had set his duffle bag. He obviously got the hint that talking about how things *used* to be around here made me uncomfortable, and I was grateful for that.

"Okay," I said as I made my way toward the door. "I'll go get dinner set out while you shower." With a nod, I turned and shut the door behind me.

Less than fifteen minutes later, John and I were sitting comfortably on one of the front porch swings. He hauled it out of the parlor, where I had stored it before the storm hit, and hung it while I was arranging dinner.

He had surprised me with the thoughtful gesture, and I appreciated it greatly as I inhaled my turkey and cheese on homemade bread. Sitting quietly while we listened to the cicadas buzz, John slowly pushed the swing back and forth with his long legs as I sat with mine curled under me. It reminded me of swinging with my grandfather as a child, when my legs were too short to reach the floor. The sweet memory brought a small smile to my face as I watched lightning bugs rise from the grass as darkness fell.

"God, this is good," John said around a mouthful of roast beef and cheese. "Either your Miss Daisy is a culinary genius or I am insanely hungry. Either way, this might be the best sandwich I've ever eaten." He wiped a crumb off of his t-shirt and let his head fall back against the swing. "What a day, huh? I can't believe how much we accomplished."

He sighed as he chewed his sandwich with his eyes closed, and I took the opportunity to study his handsome profile. His tan skin looked even darker in the glow of the lanterns I had placed on the porch railing when we came outside to eat. I knew, with no power and only a small slice of moon rising in the sky, it would get very dark, very quickly.

His long, dark eyelashes cast a shadow under his closed eyes. Why did guys always end up with such amazing eyelashes? I would need at least ten coats of mascara to achieve what God gave him naturally.

His high cheekbones and chiseled jaw gave him a classically handsome face. There was something else about him, though, that made me feel... different. I couldn't quite put my finger on it, but I knew it wasn't a reaction I had ever experienced before.

His dark hair, still damp from his shower, fell over his forehead in a messy style that made me think he had scrubbed his towel over it and didn't bother to comb it. I liked the casual vibe it gave him. It suited his relaxed character, from what I could tell.

Not wanting to get caught staring, I turned my head back to look out over the lawn. "So, John, tell me your story. What brought you over to Heartsail Island this morning?" I took another bite of my sandwich while I waited for his answer. He lifted his head and looked directly at me. "I'm starting to think it was fate, Nora." Those deep, chocolate brown eyes stared into mine when I turned to look at him, and we remained that way for a long moment.

Breaking our gaze with a wink, he took another bite of his sandwich. "Actually, I quit my job at my dad's sleazy construction firm this morning. He wanted me to go out and find storm victims he could scam out of their hard-earned money, and I refused to do it. So I just quit. I packed a bag, hopped in my boat, and came over here to see who I could actually help instead."

I looked at him in surprise. "So, you had no plan at all?" I couldn't imagine not thinking through an idea like that. Just showing up somewhere and hoping for the best? Definitely not my cup of tea!

"Nope. I'm a bit of a 'fly by the seat of my pants' kind of guy. Spontaneity makes life more interesting." He shrugged his shoulders as he finished his sandwich, then stood up from the swing. "I mean, I never would have met you if I thought things through, right?" He picked up my hand from the arm of the swing and brushed a light kiss over my knuckles. My mouth dropped open and my eyes flew to his, and he rewarded me with another of his sexy winks. "Now, if you'll excuse me, my boss is a bit of a tyrant, so I'm beat. I'm going to go pass out in that beautiful bed upstairs. Goodnight, Nora." With that, he released my hand, gathered the empty plates and one of the lanterns, and disappeared inside the inn.

What in the world had just happened?

*Chapter 9*

♥

# John

I WAS IN SO much trouble. As I sunk into the comfortable bed in my room at the inn, I replayed the scene on the front porch in my mind.

The longer I sat on that pretty porch swing, so close to Nora that I could smell her shampoo, the more I wanted to take her in my arms and kiss her. The look on Nora's face when I took her hand and pressed a light kiss to it... it almost did me in. I knew I needed to get away from her before I scared her off completely, which was why I left when I did.

I was a sucker for a damsel in distress. But that was definitely not a phrase that would describe Nora Weatherly. She was probably the most self sufficient, independent, hardworking, driven woman I had ever met.

Apparently, I was even more a sucker for that type of woman.

I had known the woman for less than twenty four hours. In that short time, however, the unexplainable pull I felt towards Nora made me want to do everything in my power to make her life easier. True, she hadn't opened up much about her life, but I definitely got the impression that things hadn't always been easy. She had obviously suffered a lot of loss for someone her age. To have the responsibility of running this inn squarely on her shoulders alone? Well, I imagined that was more than most people could handle.

And don't even get me started on how beautiful she was. Those crystal blue eyes alone were enough to send me right over the edge. Add to that the gorgeous face, curves in ALL the right places, and legs that made my mouth water? Yeah, I was a goner.

I noticed her watching me through the windows she was working on several times throughout the day. Each time, I tried to pretend that I didn't see her. I got the impression it would embarrass her if she knew I saw her. I didn't want her to feel that way, so I just kept working.

Ok, maybe I flexed a little extra, or made sure I made myself look as good as possible, but what man wouldn't want a woman like Nora to see him at his best?

As I drifted off into an exhausted sleep, I had a feeling I would dream about a certain blue eyed princess looking down at me from a castle tower.

The next several days passed in a blur of nonstop manual labor. Word of the significant damage to the deck had spread across the island like wildfire after Mayor Dobson visited to check on Nora and the inn. This news caused an outpouring of generosity from the residents of Heartsail Island. A few times a day since the mayor's visit, someone from town would show up with an offer of help with clean-up and removal of some of the debris. On multiple occasions, residents even showed up with trucks filled with building materials they "found lying around" or had "inadvertently over purchased." Nora accepted the help graciously, as any proper southern lady would, but I could see a glimmer of embarrassment in her eyes every time someone showed up with what she considered a 'handout.'

Her best friend, Beth, and her mother, Miss Daisy, came down at least once a day to make sure we were taking time from our nonstop working to eat a decent meal. Miss Daisy insisted on bringing us dinner every evening. I got the feeling that she was one of the few people who could make Nora do something she didn't want to do without an argument. And I certainly wasn't complaining, because the woman was an outstanding cook.

The marina had also restored ferry service to the island, which meant that tee times at the golf course had picked up where they left off before the storm. Harry, the manager of the course, along with two of his teenage sons, worked their tails off and got the course back in shape and ready for visitors in just two days after the storm. While there were still areas around the fairways that needed sprucing up, and some piles of debris that needed to be disposed of, golfers had returned in earnest.

Power had finally been restored to the inn as well, so I broke out the power tools to cut the lumber for the new hurricane shutters. Nora assembled and painted them to match the existing shutters, and we worked together to get them hung.

The return of electricity also meant that we could run fans in the guest rooms that had sustained water damage, and they quickly dried out enough to get the new windows installed. It pleased Nora that the floors dried out mostly smooth and stain-free, because it meant she wouldn't need to replace them. A well-placed piece of furniture would do the trick to hide any of the minor imperfections left behind from Louisa's wrath.

Besides getting a ton of work accomplished, working closely in the guest rooms with Nora over the last week had also given me the opportunity to learn more about her. And the more I learned, the more I wanted to know. The walls that she had constructed around herself were slowly coming down.

She told me about her parents, and how their untimely deaths had shaped her young life. She regaled me with stories about growing up here with her grandfather and how exciting it had always been to have the inn and beach cabins filled with visitors and staff. Even though she had suffered so much loss in her young life, she had apparently never been lonely.

Her grandfather's illness, however, had changed everything for her. When they could no longer afford to pay staff, because of his costly medical bills, the inn shut down. And Nora's world had shattered again when he passed.

Hanging the new drywall had been a two person job, but once that was done, we decided it would be faster for us to divide and conquer on the painting.

Nora had taken the room in the front of the house, and I tackled the two in the back. I was a fast painter, since I had spent an entire summer during my teens working alongside a painter on one of my dad's crews. He taught me many tricks to speed up the process, so two guest room walls were no problem at all for me.

I had been mulling over an idea the last couple of hours I spent painting, and I decided I had it fleshed out well enough to bring it up with Nora. I didn't want her to be distracted with work when I broached the subject, though, so I waited until we finished cleaning up the painting supplies to bring it up.

"Hey Nora, why don't we clock out a little early tonight? It's almost dinnertime, and we've been killing ourselves over the last week. How about a walk on the beach before Miss Daisy shows up with her latest culinary masterpiece?" I dried my hands on a towel after I finished arranging the freshly cleaned painting supplies in the small shed Nora used for maintenance equipment and tools.

Nora, however, had other plans.

# Chapter 10

♥

## Nora

I COULD TELL JUST how tired John was after the week we had just been through. If he felt anything like me, then I was ashamed to say I had massively overworked him.

When he suggested we take the evening off and go for a walk on the beach, an idea popped into my head and I ran with it before I changed my mind.

"Nope. No walk on the beach. I'm going to call Miss Daisy and cancel her daily dinner delivery, then we're going into town to celebrate."

"Celebrate?" His raised eyebrows showed his surprise at my spontaneous suggestion. "What, exactly, are we celebrating?"

I stepped out of the stuffy maintenance shed, lifted my face to the sky, and threw my hands out wide. "Everything. Our progress on the inn, that the golf course is open again, just... everything." I turned and smiled at John as he pushed the shed door closed behind him. "I don't think I have really told you how grateful I am for all of your help this past week. There is no way I would have been able to accomplish even a portion of what we did this week without your help. Truly. Thank you." Before I let my brain talk me out of it, I stepped forward and threw my arms around his neck in a tight hug. After a second of hesitation, his arms circled my waist, and he hugged me back.

"It was my pleasure, Nora." His quiet voice was like a caress over me as we stood in the embrace. I pulled back just a little and looked up into his gorgeous brown eyes.

It hadn't escaped my attention that John got a certain look in his eye when we had worked closely together over the previous week. There was obviously an attraction there. And the longer we were around each other, the more my feelings toward him were becoming less 'business' and more 'personal.' There was no doubt in my mind that, if I remained where I was for much longer, he was going to kiss me.

I wasn't one hundred percent sure I was ready, or willing, to cross that line yet, however, so I stepped back out of the hug. Intent on lightening the mood, I turned and ran towards the inn. "Last one ready to go buys dinner!" I called over my shoulder, and I could hear him laugh as I ran.

Of course, John had been ready to go long before I was, so I had treated him to dinner at Dobson's Cafe in town. He fought me on it, as I assumed he would, but it had always been my intention to pay, so I didn't let him win.

Ok, so maybe I took a few extra minutes to make sure I styled my long, light brown hair in more than just my normal ponytail, that my favorite sundress hugged my curves in just the right way, and the small amount of makeup I applied looked as natural as possible. And maybe I called Beth from my room to make sure we could have a table outside so we could enjoy the evening breeze. And to ask if she could set aside a piece of Miss Daisy's blackberry cheesecake, which had quickly become John's favorite dessert. But, hey! We were celebrating, right? And John definitely seemed to appreciate what he saw when I finally made my way out of my room and onto the front porch where he sat on the swing waiting for me.

It was nice to relax and let go of some worries and stress I had been carrying ever since Hurricane Louisa had hit. I didn't realize just how tense I had been. Now that I was strolling through the town square as the sun sank low in the sky with a takeout cup filled with Miss Daisy's sweet tea, however, my body was practically sighing in relief.

"Besides the day I arrived and a few quick trips to the hardware store, I haven't really had time to come into town and look around. I'm glad we are taking the evening off to enjoy it. It's so beautiful. You're lucky to live in a place like this," John said. I looked around the pretty town square as he spoke. It didn't surprise me how quickly everyone had pulled together to get it cleaned up and looking good as new after the storm. Looking around, you might never even know it had been a terrible mess just a week ago.

"You're not wrong," I said as we strolled through the grass. "I've had some really hard times in my life, but the people of this island have always been there for me. When my mom died, the Dobson's stepped in and were like my surrogate parents. And when I lost Gramps? Well, you should have seen the beautiful memorial that everyone helped arrange as a celebration of his life. I was so heartbroken. I had no idea where to even begin planning something like that. But this town pulled together and got me through the worst of it. They even commissioned a memorial bench in his memory. It's over on the boardwalk near the pier. He loved it there. Besides the inn, the pier was one of his favorite places on the whole island. I go there sometimes just to sit and see the little plaque with his name on it. It makes me feel like he is still with me."

John was quiet for a moment while we walked down a residential street that led to the boardwalk and pier. I couldn't really tell if my confession made him feel uncomfortable or just thoughtful. I had a tendency to keep most of my deeper thoughts to myself, so in the short time we'd known each other, I had never really shared anything so personal with him. But when he reached down and took my hand, and placed it in the bend of his elbow, I was pretty sure I hadn't made him too uncomfortable.

"Can I confess something to you, Nora?" he asked. His brown eyes peered into mine, and I nodded my head silently. "I am completely in awe of you. Even though you've lost so much, at such a young age, you know exactly who you are and where you belong. This island is your place, and the residents are your people. And there is no doubt in my mind that you will make an unbridled success of the inn. You, Nora Weatherly, are incredible."

I was at a total loss for words as we arrived at the boardwalk. We continued to walk in silence as we neared the pier. It was a beautiful evening, so it wasn't a surprise to see so many of the island residents out for a stroll. Ice cream and snack vendors did brisk business. There were even still some die-hard beach goers sprinkled around the sand on either side of the pier.

John really believed I would be a successful innkeeper? His faith in me took me completely by surprise. I never really gave myself permission to consider myself a success. I spent so much time focused on what I still needed to accomplish to reflect on all the things I've already accomplished. But hearing John say he was in awe of me? That was a huge shock.

As we reached the end of the pier, I turned to John, stretched up onto my toes, and placed a light kiss on his cheek. "Thank you, John," I whispered. I leaned my head on his shoulder and we stood looking out over the ocean.

*Chapter 11*

♥

# John

OUR EVENING IN TOWN last night still
played in my mind. Over and over, I relived
the feel of Nora's soft lips against my cheek. It had
taken all of my willpower not to scoop her up in
my arms and kiss her until we both forgot where
we were.

Every day we had spent together, I could feel us
growing closer and closer. I knew she felt the same,
but I also knew I shouldn't push her before I was
sure she was ready to take that step.

As I sat in the sand, replaying our evening once
again, I rolled my shoulders to release the knot
that had been present for the last few days.
Between the physical labor and emotional tension
I'd been through over the last week, it surprised
me I could even swing a hammer anymore.

We had spent the day piling, cutting, and
disposing of the rest of the debris from the deck.
To say that it had been a physically taxing day was
an understatement. I knew that, technically, our
original agreement had come to its natural
conclusion. The repairs that Nora and I had agreed

to were all finished. She was ready to reschedule her soft 'friends and family' opening. And I needed to prepare myself to move on from Heartsail Inn.

But an idea that had been forming in my head over the last few days might just be the answer to my prayers. I had planned on bringing it up with her last night, but the right moment never presented itself. I knew the time had finally come, however, that I needed to broach the subject with Nora. I was really curious about how she would react to the idea. I prayed she thought it was a good one.

Nora approached the two beach chairs I dug out of the storage shed with two glasses of sweet tea and a smile. "Hey," I said, as she handed me a glass and plopped in the chair beside mine.

"What a day," she said, leaning back in the chair with her eyes closed. "I'm so happy we finished cleaning up all that mess. I can't wait to take my re-opening paperwork into town for approval. It will be so great to have some guests around here again. Besides you, of course."

A gull let out a cry as it flew overhead, and Nora smiled, her eyes still closed. "I don't think I've ever worked harder in my entire life that we did in the last week," she said. She turned her head and peeked through her heavy eyelids at me. "I really want to thank you, John. I never would have been able to accomplish all of this without you. Especially not so quickly."

Since she had just provided me with the perfect opening, I knew it was time to tell her about my idea. I took a large gulp of tea and turned in my chair to face her. "Nora," I said, "there's something I've been meaning to talk to you about. When I came here, our agreement was for me to help you fix the storm damage in exchange for a place to stay. I'm pretty sure, unless there was something else you didn't tell me about, we've both fulfilled our ends of the deal."

I paused for a moment to judge her reaction to my statement, and I had to admit I was a little relieved to see disappointment flash across her beautiful face. That small reaction was all I needed to give me the courage to tell her about my idea.

"Now that we're finished, you have every right to send me on my way," I said. "But what if we amended our original agreement instead?"

Nora raised her eyebrows at the question. "What, exactly, did you have in mind?" she asked. It was exactly the question I had hoped she would ask.

"I've been thinking about it a lot over the last few days, and I decided that I'm going to stay here on Heartsail Island. There's nothing for me to go back to on the mainland. I really love it here. This island feels like home to me," I said. I reached out and took her hand in mine and turned to look toward the inn. "This inn, this island... it is all so special. And I want to be a part of it. So, what would you say to me staying on as an employee? Indefinitely." I swallowed deeply and hoped that she would think it was a good idea.

Nora looked down at our joined hands. "John, I am so grateful for everything you have done for me. Like I said, I never would have been able to do it without you. But there is no way I can take on an employee right now. I haven't even opened to guests yet, and the golf course only brings in enough income to pay Harry at this point."

I had a feeling this would be her initial response, so I had already thought of how I would counter. "What if I said you didn't have to pay me? Not at first, at least. What if I continued to work here in exchange for room and board? I could work to fix up one of the beach cabins, so you could rent out the room I've been staying in. And then I could help you get the place up and running. I could take care of any maintenance issues that come up, and you could focus all your time and attention on your guests." She looked conflicted, so I continued.

"You can't possibly run this place all on your own, Nora. Even though you are the most amazingly capable woman I have ever met, you are going to need some help. I'm offering to be that help. I want to be that help." I squeezed her hand, conveying my desire for her to agree.

"John, I can't ask you to work for free," she said, shaking her head with a frown. "I would feel like I'm taking advantage of you."

"Nora, as long as I have a roof over my head and food to eat, that's all I need at this point. I have savings I can live off of for a few months until you book guests with regularity. And besides," I said with one of my famous half-smiles, "you aren't asking. I'm offering. Please, Nora? Let's help each other again. It worked out so well the first time. I just know it will keep working."

She sat quietly for a moment, staring out over the ocean. I could tell she was struggling with the idea. I squeezed her hand again and a small smile curved up on her beautiful lips.

"Let's do it," she said with a nod. I let out a whoop as I jumped out of my chair and pulled her into my arms. I spun in a circle and we both laughed as we celebrated.

Without even thinking about it, I hitched Nora over my shoulder and ran straight into the crashing waves.

*Chapter 12*

♥

# Nora

THE COOL OCEAN WATER shocked my over-heated skin when John dumped me off of his shoulder into the salty sea. I came up, sputtering and laughing, as I pushed my wet hair out of my face. My clothes clung to my body, probably giving him more of a show than I intended when I dressed this morning.

John was laughing and splashing around in the waves like a small child. The utter joy on his face made my heart grow. His wet t-shirt clung to him like a second skin, showing off his muscular chest and arms. My mouth watered at the sight. Goodness, this man was everything I had ever dreamed of in my young life.

Without giving myself the chance to overthink, I pushed myself through the water toward him. Surprise showed on his face as I placed my hands on his biceps. His laughter stopped, and he stilled as hands came to my waist. For a long beat, we stood, eyes locked, as the waves rose and fell around us. He didn't pull me into his body. I could see the desire in his eyes, but still he held himself back.

I was done holding back, however. Slowly, I rose up on my toes, and used the buoyancy of the water to help me reconcile for our height difference. As I slid my hands up around his shoulders, his grip tightened around my waist. He pulled my body flush against his, my feet rising slightly off the ocean floor. Eyes still locked, I moved in closer until my lips were just a whisper away from his.

"Nora," he whispered, looking deeply into my eyes, "This will change things. Are you sure?" Without a word, my eyelids fluttered closed, and I eliminated the distance between our lips.

I had never really been much of a 'dater' in the past. Sure, I had kissed a few guys in high school, but nothing serious. Beth had always described the kisses with her many boyfriends in terms of fireworks and explosions.

That was *not* what I felt when my lips finally met John's, though.

I felt molten lava. My lips, my body, my soul became hot and fluid. John's lips moved slowly and softly over mine like warm, smooth honey. He lifted me higher, held my body even tighter to his. I wrapped my legs around his narrow waist as the ocean waves continued to ebb and flow around us.

John's tongue parted my lips, and I could taste the combination of sweet tea and salt water. One of his strong, rough hands slid up my back and into my wet hair as the other continued to hold me tightly around the waist. The feeling of his palm on the exposed skin of my upper back as it made its journey upward made me gasp with a shiver.

The kiss wasn't rushed or desperate. It felt more like worship - like John was taking his time to savor every taste, every sigh, every moment. I felt like a goddess. I could practically imagine rays of golden light shooting out from our entwined bodies. It was the most exhilarating and powerful feeling I had ever experienced.

John's lips traced a path down the column of my neck, to the curve of my collarbone. I raised my face to the sky, eyes still closed, as I savored the feeling of his lips on my hot, wet skin.

When his lips traveled back up to mine, the kiss became deeper, more urgent. I tightened my legs around his waist, pushing our bodies even closer to one another. John's tongue tangled with mine as our hands tangled in one another's hair.

I had no idea how long we remained locked in our embrace, as time had become insignificant. All that mattered right now was this feeling. All that mattered was that I was in the arms of the most incredible man I had ever met, and that he was in mine. I never wanted this feeling to end.

When the kiss ebbed, John rested his forehead on mine, our eyes still closed, bodies still pressed together. "Nora," he whispered again, "you have no idea how long I have been dying to do that."

I let out a small chuckle as I pulled my forehead back from his and opened my eyes. "Boy, are we dumb," I said with a laugh. "Me, too. We sure wasted a ton of time."

He smiled his sexy half-smile at me before closing the distance between us again. "Well, not anymore," he said as he brought his lips back to mine for another soul-melting kiss.

Apparently, sometime during our ocean make-out session, Beth had stopped by the inn without our knowledge. When we finally came up for air and made our way back up to the sand, we found a basket of food, a bottle of wine, and a beach blanket folded on the chairs we had been sitting in earlier.

Long after the sun had set and the stars twinkled in the black night sky, John and I snuggled together, wrapped in the blanket on the still-warm sand. Now that we had crossed the line from friends to *'more than friends,'* it appeared neither one of us had any intention of going back to the way things were.

For hours, John and I had lounged on the blanket, alternating between talking, kissing, touching, and gazing quietly at the stars. I had no idea what time it was, but the inky black sky told me it was late. Now, as we dozed in each other's arms - my head resting on his chest, our legs entwined - his strong arms held me tightly to his body.

I had never felt so relaxed or at ease in my entire life. I couldn't pinpoint the exact moment it happened during our incredible evening, but I realized that this was exactly what I wanted for my life. This place, this man, this feeling... I knew John was my person, and that I was his. I knew we were meant to be. Here, on Heartsail Island. Together. Forever.

I had fallen head-over-heels in love with this man. Now I just needed to find out if he felt the same way.

## Chapter 13

♥

# John

I N THE DAYS FOLLOWING our first kiss, I noticed a seismic shift in Nora. She seemed more open, more willing to share intimate details about her life. And the best part? She smiled more. A smile almost always graced her beautiful face now, and it warmed my heart every time I saw it.

Until that day in the waves, I had struggled to keep my hands and lips to myself. I didn't want to scare her off by crossing a line she wasn't comfortable crossing. But when she took matters into her own hands, *ohhh*, it had been worth the wait.

The moment she touched her beautiful lips to mine, as the waves rose and fell around us... well, I knew.

I just knew.

As cheesy and cliche as it might sound, I knew I had found my soul mate. I didn't want to scare her off by announcing my intentions too quickly, but I was going to marry this woman. I wanted it all with Nora. A family, the inn, a happily ever after... all of it. Yes, we were young, but that didn't mean I wasn't sure we were going to spend the rest of our lives together.

Nora applied for her reopening permit a few days ago, so we had spent the last several days preparing one of the beach cabins for me to move in. It had been a while since any of them welcomed guests, so there was a lot of work that needed to be done.

I pulled my truck into a space in the small parking lot near the hardware store. My buddy, Jeremy, had brought it over on the ferry for me earlier in the week, so I no longer needed to borrow Nora's for supply runs. This trip into town would, hopefully, be the last before I could give up my room for paying guests and move into the cabin.

As I hopped out of the truck, it surprised me to see Mayor Dobson heading my way. The look on his face made me pause mid-wave. It didn't look like he had good news.

"Good morning, John," he said as he reached out to shake my hand. "I'm glad I ran into you. Do you have a minute to talk?" Even though I was eager to get my mission completed, I nodded.

"Is everything okay?" I asked, as the two of us walked down the sidewalk toward Dobson's Cafe. I could tell by the tension that was radiating off of the usually cheerful man that he was dealing with a pretty serious problem.

"No, John. Actually, everything is not okay," he answered. He motioned toward a chair at one of the little tables outside of the cafe. As we sat, Beth, who was watering the pretty potted flowers, came over.

"Daddy, you look upset. What's wrong?" she asked as she placed a hand on her father's shoulder.

"Yeah, what's going on, sir?" I didn't have a good feeling about whatever the mayor was about to tell us.

He pulled on the knot of his tie to loosen it as he slumped back in his chair. "I just left a meeting with the building inspector and the head of the town council. Unfortunately, despite my objections, they are going to deny Nora's application to reopen the inn. I won't go into specifics. Simply put, without rebuilding the deck, the inn doesn't have enough exits to meet the fire and safety occupancy codes. I did everything I could, but they can't make an exception." He sighed and scrubbed a hand over his face. "I convinced them not to make y'all leave, too, because technically no one should be allowed to stay there. They reluctantly agreed not to force y'all out, but until she rebuilds the deck, she can't reopen."

Having watched my father skirt building codes my whole life, I understood the town council's point of view. With no exits on the back of the inn, it definitely posed a hazard. The doors were unusable for egress in an emergency, because they were a good ten feet off the ground.

Anger flooded through me as I realized the implications of what Mayor Dobson was saying. Without guests, Nora couldn't fix the deck. Without the deck, Nora couldn't have guests. I couldn't believe the thought hadn't occurred to me that this would be a problem.

"But, Daddy, Nora can't afford to fix the deck until she can bring in paying guests." Beth voiced the thought that was bouncing around in my brain. "Isn't there anything y'all can do? Can guests sign a waiver or something?"

Mayor Dobson scrubbed a hand over his face again. "I'm afraid not, honey. It's just too risky. If something happened, and a guest got injured - or worse - because they couldn't get out of the inn safely, Nora would be liable. It's just not a risk anyone should take. The inspector and town council are making the right call."

"We have to help her. This is Nora's dream. Her legacy. It's the only thing she has left of her grandfather. We can't let her down." I looked Mayor Dobson in the eye, and I could tell he felt my determination. There was no way I was going to let Nora's dream slip away because of a permitting issue. I didn't know how, but I was going to make this problem go away, even if I had to sell everything I owned to get the money for the deck.

A smile spread across Beth's face, and a glimmer of hope bloomed inside me. "I've got it! What about a fundraiser? We could ask the whole town to pitch in to help raise the money. I mean, think about it. The entire town will benefit when the inn opens back up. Tourism will increase, which means business for all of us will increase as well." Her blonde ponytail bounced in excitement as she turned between me and her father.

"I don't know, sweetie. You know how proud Nora is. She probably wouldn't be comfortable

asking for help from her friends and neighbors."
Mayor Dobson looked skeptical.

"What if we didn't tell her?" I said. I knew it was a
risk, and when Nora finally found out - and of
course she would find out - she would be livid. But
it was a risk I had to take... for the sake of Nora's
future.

# Chapter 14

♥

## Nora

WHISTLING. I WAS ACTUALLY *whistling* as I hopped out of my truck. Thanks to the bustling business of the golf course, I had a payment for Sam for the windows. Add to that, John and I were connecting on levels I had never even dreamed possible, and as soon as I got my approved permits, I was ready to reopen the inn.

The day was beautiful, for once the South Carolina humidity wasn't terribly oppressive, and the sun smiled down like a giant ball of happiness from the sky.

Could life get any better than this? I was pretty sure it couldn't!

I pushed open the door of the hardware store, and the little bell above my head let out its pretty little chime. "One second, I'll be right there, y'all!" The call came from the back room, so I meandered over to the counter.

"Take your time, Sam," I called back. "It's just me, Nora. I'm here with a payment for my windows."

Sam came scurrying out of the back. "Miss Nora! Oh, hi, darlin', how are you? I wasn't expecting you!"

"Hey Sam. I have some money here to put toward my windows. What is this for?" I asked, picking up a jar with the words DECK FUND written in large letters. Loose change and bills, ranging from pennies to twenties, filled the jar.

Sam seemed flustered as he reached out and grabbed the jar out of my hands. "Oh, that's nothing, dear. Just a little fundraiser I've been helping with for the last few days." He stowed the jar under the counter with a strange look on his face.

"Oh, that's so nice of you! Let me help." I rustled around in my purse and pulled out a few crumpled up dollar bills. "Here, stick these in there. Who is it for, anyway?" I loved that this island always came together to help a neighbor in need.

Sam's face turned bright red when I waved the bills at him. "Um," he sputtered, apparently unable to look me in the eye. "No, Miss Nora, please. Keep your money, darlin'."

I narrowed my eyes at Sam. Something weird was definitely going on, and I was beginning to think that I was being kept in the dark about something.

"Sam," I said, leveling a stare at him, "what is going on here? Who is the deck fundraiser for?" I put my hands on my hips and glared at the man, who looked like he was ready to crawl under the counter with the jar to hide.

"Oh, Miss Nora. I'm sorry, it was supposed to be a secret. The fundraiser is for you, darlin'."

My eyes grew wide in horror. For me? Who in the world would think that I would need a fundraiser? I was a strong, independent woman! I didn't need the residents of Heartsail Island to bail me out and pay for my deck!

"Sam," I said, my voice brimming with anger, "whose idea was this?" Although, I had a feeling I already knew the answer to my question.

"Well, don't be mad, Miss Nora, but your young friend John dropped this off a few days ago."

I slapped the envelope with my window payment onto the counter and stormed out of the hardware store without another word.

Anger pulsed through my body as I stomped down the sidewalk toward Dobson's Cafe. I needed to calm myself down a bit before I went back to the inn and tore the hide right off of John Franklin. What right did he have to go behind my back and have my friends and neighbors thinking I was some kind of charity case? None! And when I saw him, I was going to let him know, in no uncertain terms, where he could shove his charity!

I pushed into the cafe, sure that there was actually visible steam rising from my body. As I made my way over to a stool at the counter, I saw Beth at the cash register.

A surprised look showed on her pretty face, and I saw her reach out and grab something off the counter and stick it underneath.

My jaw dropped in dismay, and I stormed over to the register where she was finishing up with a customer.

"What did you just put behind the counter, Beth?" I demanded. But she didn't need to tell me. I knew exactly what she had put back there. "Beth, how could you?" I asked when a guilty look washed over her pretty features. "You knew about this little stunt, and didn't tell me? How could you!" I asked again.

"I am so embarrassed! You are supposed to be my best friend. How could you let John make everyone on this island think I'm some kind of charity case? You know how much I hate feeling like people feel sorry for me! You should have told me." An angry tear escaped the corner of my eye and my hand shot up to wipe it away before it could roll down my cheek. I was making a fool of myself, shouting at her in the middle of the cafe. Customers were looking on with guilt on their faces. I knew most of them, and I knew that most of them had probably stuffed money in the very jar that Beth had just hidden.

"Nora, we were just trying to help. When Daddy said you wouldn't be able to reopen the inn without rebuilding the deck, we had to do something."

"Wait, what did you just say?" I asked, dread suddenly filling my entire body. "What do you mean, I won't be able to reopen the inn?" My hands shook, the combination of adrenaline, anger, and fear threatening to overtake me. I looked around and saw every set of eyes in the place trained on the two of us. The entire cafe had grown silent. Mortification overwhelmed me. I saw nothing but pity in those eyes, and I wanted to crawl behind the counter to hide with that stupid little jar of bills.

Beth came out from behind the counter, took my hand, and led me into the more private kitchen area of the cafe. "Nora, Daddy told John and me a few days ago that the town council wouldn't approve your permit to reopen if you didn't rebuild the deck. It has something to do with fire codes and emergency exit regulations. We thought this would be the easiest way to help you get the money for the deck. I'm sorry we didn't tell you, Nora."

She looked at me with so much pity in her eyes. I didn't know what to do besides turn on my heels and run out of the cafe without a word.

As I drove the short distance from town back down to the inn, my embarrassment had plenty of time to return to rage. I slammed the truck in park and got out. I knew exactly where he would be, so I headed toward the beach cabin he was refurbishing to rip the hide off of John for this stunt.

Music filled my ears as I pushed the door open with enough force to have it slamming against the wall.

"How dare you?" I yelled, and the paintbrush that had been in his hand clattered to the tarp covering the floor. "You hand NO right to go behind my back and treat me like some kind of charity case!"

"Nora, let me explain," he said, coming over and reaching for my hands. But I didn't want to hear his explanation. I jerked my hands away from him, stiffened my spine, and narrowed my eyes at him.

"No. No explanation is necessary. You didn't believe that I could do this on my own. You didn't even have the decency to tell me about the problems with the permit. This is MY business, John. *Mine*. You have no right to come in here and start making decisions for me. You are just the hired help, remember? I'm the boss. I own this place, and I am the only one who should decide how to run it. *NOT YOU!*"

"But Nora, you won't be able to--"

I cut him off with a glare. "*NO!*" I shouted. "I don't want to hear your explanations. You're fired. Get your stuff and get out. Now. I never want to see your face on my property again."

And with that, I turned around and slammed the door closed on my future with John Franklin.

# Chapter 15

♥

# John

I SAT ON THE ferry, completely stunned by what had just happened. Nora hated me. That was plain to see. The look on her face, the anger I could feel coming off her in waves. I was pretty sure she would never forgive me.

I had called Jeremy from the marina before I left the island. I had packed up all of my stuff and quickly left the inn, but I left it all in the cab of my truck on Heartsail Island. Bringing my truck back over to the mainland had seemed too... final.

Jeremy had agreed to meet me at the ferry dock, and when I stepped off the ferry and back on to the mainland, my spirits plummeted even further.

"Brother, you look like crap," he said, clapping a hand on my shoulder. "Let's go get a drink, and you can tell me what is so awful that you made me take a day away from the pool to come and pick your sorry butt up."

Jeremy's job as a fifth grade teacher gave him flexibility during the summer months, and for that I was glad, especially when I really needed a shoulder to lean on.

We climbed into his car and headed inland a few miles before he pulled over at a small dive bar along the side of the road. Despite the beautiful sunshine of the day, the bar looked just about right for my current mood. Run down, dark, and dreary.

My feet felt heavy, like they were encased in concrete, as we made our way into the darkness of the bar's interior. It took a moment for my eyes to adjust to the change in light, but when they did, my suspicions were confirmed. Depressing was the only word I could use to describe the interior of the joint. Sad looking people sat at grimy tables, and a sad country song moaned out from the fingerprint-covered jukebox in the corner.

"Whadda y'all want?" the surly bartender snarled as we sat on stools at the empty bar. He replied to Jeremy's request for two of whatever he had on tap with a grunt and turned away to pull the pints.

"So, you ready to tell me what's up?" Jeremy eyed me with suspicion. I knew, between the two of us, I was usually the more carefree friend. Jeremy was much more serious with goals and ambitions. He had gone to college and became a teacher, while I had gone to work for my dad's company. He always worried I would regret it, and said I should have a backup plan, but I never really felt a calling toward any particular career like he did to teaching.

Now, I wished I had listened to him, because, once again, I had no idea what I was going to do with my life.

"Nora hates me." I took a long drink of the beer that the bartender had put in front of me. When I didn't elaborate, Jeremy punched me lightly on the shoulder.

"I'm gonna need a little more info, buddy," he said, trying to lighten the mood. But there was no lightening the mood for me. My heart was completely broken.

"Yeah, okay." I put my beer down on the bar and leaned forward with my head in my hands. Before I knew what was happening, my mouth started moving and the entire story poured out of me like water from a faucet. "So, you know I told you that the hurricane destroyed Nora's deck? Well, turns out she doesn't have the money to replace it right now. But the town council decided they wouldn't approve her permits until she did. Code violations, they said. And I get it. So, her friend Beth and I started a fundraiser to help replace the deck so she could reopen. But we didn't tell her about it, because we knew she wouldn't agree to it. But today she found out about it, and she was beyond mad. Irate, if I were to use one of your fancy words. She told me I had no right to do what I did, and that I had embarrassed her in front of the entire island. She fired me and told me to get off her property and that she never wants to see me again. Nora hates me, Jer." I took another long sip of beer. "I am completely in love with her, and she hates me."

Jeremy sat quietly for a moment, apparently trying to take in everything I had just dumped on him. "Okay, let me get this straight. You were trying to help her reopen her inn, and she got mad at you for going behind her back with a fundraiser. That sound about right?"

I nodded my head.

"Well, it sounds to me like you screwed up, bro. I know I haven't met her, but it seems like she is very proud and likes to do things on her own. By sneaking around and asking people to help her without her knowledge, you betrayed her trust."

I ran my finger down the side of my glass. "I know I did. She should have been told about the fundraiser. But I didn't think she would go along with it, and it was the only way I could think of to help her open as quickly as possible."

"So, what are you going to do about it?"

I turned and looked at my best friend. "What do you mean? There's nothing I CAN do. She hates me. She told me to leave and never come back. I lost her. I love her, but I lost her."

Jeremy carefully sat his beer down on the bar and shook his head. "I'm disappointed in you, John."

"Seriously? After everything I've been through, you're going to turn on me too?" I stood up from the stool and prepared to storm out. How could Jeremy say something like that? I was hurting, and he was supposed to be on my side. But apparently, I was just a loser all the way around.

"John, stop." Jeremy reached out and grabbed my arm before I could leave. "I didn't mean it that way. What I meant was, I'm disappointed that you are giving up so easily. Do you really love Nora?"

"Yes. I really do."

"And do you want to help her succeed with the inn?"

"Again, yes."

Jeremy slapped me on the back with a huge smile on his face. "Then what the heck are you doing sitting here in this dive with me? Get your butt back over to that island and fix what you broke."

I looked at Jeremy, and I suddenly realized that he was right. I had to fix this. My heart belonged to Nora, and I belonged on Heartsail Island.

"You are so right, Jeremy. I need to call Beth and figure out a way to get Nora to forgive me." I stood up from my stool again and gave Jeremy a back-slapping man hug.

"Hey, barkeep! Y'all got a payphone in this joint?" Jeremy asked the grumpy bartender.

"On the wall by the door," he grunted. "And don't call my bar a dive."

# Chapter 16

♥

## Nora

"I KNOW YOU'RE STILL mad at me, but this is my way of apologizing. Daddy feels horrible that he didn't come to you first with the permit issues. He paid for the entire weekend. Let's just forget about the real world for a few days, and let someone else take care of us for a change."

Beth pleaded her case as she drove her cute little car off the ferry and headed toward Charleston. I'm still not exactly sure how I let her talk me into this, because I was still furious at her for the stunt she and John had pulled. But, in a way that only Beth could manage, she had convinced me to go with her to Charleston for a girls' weekend. Okay, so a weekend getaway at a posh spa in the city did sound like a good way to relax and let go of my stress for a little while, but that didn't mean I wasn't still mad as a hornet.

I wasn't quite ready to let Beth off the hook, however. "Beth, I still can't believe you and John did that to me. I am so embarrassed. Now the entire island thinks I am incapable of running my business without handouts. How will I ever be taken seriously as a business owner if I can't run things on my own without my boyfriend, my best friend, and her father, the mayor, stepping in and fixing them for me?"

I pulled at a loose hem on the skirt of my sundress as Beth flexed her hands on the steering wheel. "Nora, I really am sorry. We didn't intend to embarrass you, I promise. And the whole thing was my idea. Not John's. Okay, so maybe he was the one who suggested that we not tell you about it right away, but he was just trying to help. He knew you would say no. He really cares about you, though. All we were trying to do was make it possible for you to get your permits as fast as possible. Everyone knows what an amazing and self-sufficient woman you are. We just wanted to help. I love you, Nora. The entire island loves you. And I'm pretty sure John loves you, too. In fact, I think he's probably *in* love with you."

I closed my eyes and rested my head on the headrest. Did she really think he was in love with me? Could that even be possible? I mean, we hadn't even known each other for a full month yet. But I'd be lying if I didn't admit that I was probably in love with him, too. My feelings for him had come on so strong and so suddenly... it very well could be love.

And yet, I sent him away.

How could I have let my anger get so out of control? As fast and strong as it had come on, it was dissipating just as fast when I took a step back and realized Beth and John were only trying to help me.

They didn't set out to embarrass me... their only goal had been to make my life easier.

And I sent him away.

"Did I ruin everything, Beth?" I asked quietly. "I fired him. And I kicked him out. He probably hates me for the way I spoke to him." I turned my head to watch the scenery pass as we cruised toward the city.

"Nora," Beth said, as she reached over and took my hand, "I'm sure he will forgive you if you ask him to come back. But let's not think about it right now. We'll be at the spa soon, and we will burn a hole in Daddy's credit card. All the pampering will help you get some perspective on the situation, and then you can figure out how to get John to come back to you."

We spent the entire weekend wrapped in fluffy robes. Beth hadn't been kidding when she said her dad was treating us to anything we wanted. I had been buffed, rubbed, polished, and pampered more in the past two days than I had ever been in my life.

As the ferry arrived back on Heartsail Island, I could still feel the aftereffects of the relaxing weekend. My limbs felt loose, my soul felt light. I knew that the very first thing I would do the moment I arrived home would be to pick up the phone and call John.

The thought of how the conversation would go, however, had me tensing up a bit. Could he forgive my behavior? Would he be willing to come back to the inn? Would he be willing to come back to ME?

"What's going on in that pretty little head of yours, Nora?" Beth asked as we headed out of town toward the inn. "You're picking at your brand new manicure, girl. Now, spill."

I turned my head toward her and smiled. She knew me so well. "I'm just a little nervous, I guess. I told you, I'm going to call John as soon as I get home, and I'm a little anxious about how he will react. That's all."

Beth reached over and patted my knee. "You worry too much, sweetie. I'm sure everything is going to work out exactly as it should."

Beth pulled her little car into the drive and stopped right in front of the walkway leading to the front porch. "Mind if I pop inside for a minute and grab a quick drink of water? The drive left me a little parched." She turned off the car and hopped out while I pulled my bag from the back seat.

"Sure," I said. "And maybe you could stick around and be my emotional support in case John tells me to go jump in the ocean during my apology."

Beth wrapped her arm around my shoulder and squeezed. "I think you're going to be quite happy with the way everything works out."

We stepped up on the porch, her much more optimistic than me, when suddenly, the front door opened and John was standing right in front of me.

"I'll just give you two some privacy," Beth said with a wink, and she disappeared into the house behind him.

## Chapter 17

♥

## John

NORA'S FACE SHOWED HER surprise at finding me standing in the inn's door.

"Hi, Nora," I said quietly.

Her mouth opened and closed a few times before any words actually formed. "John, you're here," she finally said.

"Yes, I'm here. But before you say anything, I have something to tell you. If you want to kick me out again, I understand. But you said your piece. Now I need to say mine."

I stepped forward and took the overnight bag strap off her shoulder and placed it gently on the floor. Then I took her hands in mine.

"Nora, I know you're mad at me for not telling you about the permits. And also for going behind your back and arranging the fundraiser. And I totally respect that. But please, let me explain why I did it the way I did."

I led her over to the swing, and we sat down. "I should have come to you right away when Mayor Dobson told me about the problems with the permit. But you have had so much on your plate for so long... well... I just wanted to help you. Beth said you would be upset if we told you about organizing a fundraiser, so it was totally my idea to keep it a secret. You shouldn't be mad at her."

"John..." Nora said, but I held up my hand and cut her off before she could continue. I needed to get it all out before she sent me on my way again.

"Wait, let me finish. Please. Nora, the people of this island love you. They consider you family. And they would do anything to help you. Would you come with me for a minute, please? I have something I want to show you."

I took her hand and led her into the inn, down the hallway to the kitchen, and to the back door. "Please don't be mad, Nora," I said as I opened the door.

Nora's mouth dropped open as I led her out on to the newly completed deck. Her eyes filled with tears as she looked around and saw many of her neighbors, including Mayor Dobson and Sam from the hardware store, as well as many others. Miss Daisy and Beth stood next to a table filled with snacks and drinks.

"This is my friend, Jeremy." I motioned to Jeremy, and he reached out to shake Nora's hand. "He came over to help, along with everyone else here. It was a total group effort. We all care about you, Nora, and want to see this inn succeed."

Silent tears spilled down Nora's cheeks as I stood next to her, waiting for her reaction. I started to get worried when she didn't say anything, but then she turned to me and threw her arms around my neck. She pressed her lips to mine as my arms hugged her body close. It was then that I knew my grand gesture had paid off.

After what seemed like both just a second and an eternity, Mayor Dobson stepped forward and cleared his throat.

"Nora," he said, after we parted, "you are like a daughter to me. Daisy, Beth, and I love you more than you will ever know. This entire island loves you. And it NEEDS this inn." He pulled a folded piece of paper out of his back pocket and handed it to her. "This beautiful new deck passed inspection with flying colors. Here is your approved permit. It is my great pleasure to inform you that, effective immediately, Heartsail Inn may officially re-open for business."

A sob escaped Nora's mouth as Mayor Dobson gathered her in for a hug. Beth and Miss Daisy joined, and both had tears streaming down their faces as well.

"You did good, brother," Jeremy said as he placed a hand on my shoulder. "I can see why you love it here so much. This place is special." He cut a quick gaze toward Beth and then whispered in my ear. "I may have to spend a little more time here myself."

I laughed at my best friend as I slung an arm around his shoulder. "I would be a liar if I said I hadn't considered the two of you hitting it off."

We spent the next few hours in a haze of happiness and celebration. Nora floated from guest to guest, making sure they knew just how appreciative she was for all of their help and support. I stood back, giving her the time and space she needed. I knew she had forgiven me, but what I didn't know was if she was ready to take the next step in our relationship. But to find out, I would need some privacy.

The moon had risen over the waves as I stood with my back to the party. At some point, someone had turned music on, and people were dancing and enjoying themselves. I took a pull from my beer, then turned when I felt a hand slide up my bicep to my shoulder.

"Hey." Nora stood next to me, her eyes sparkling in the moonlight. "Can we talk?"

I sat my bottle on the railing and took her hand in mine. "Sure," I said. "How about a walk on the beach?"

She nodded in agreement, and the two of us went down the steps that led to the walkway through the dunes. We both remained quiet until we reached the sand.

"John, I need to apologize to you. I shouldn't have reacted the way I did the other day. You were trying to help me, and I was so awful to you." A stray tear slid down her cheek. I reached out and brushed it away with the pad of my thumb, then gathered her in my arms.

"No, Nora. You were right to be mad. I should have come to you as soon as I learned about the permit problems. We shouldn't have gone behind your back. We just wanted to help."

Nora nodded her head. "I know, John. I get that now. But everything you and the residents of this island did to help me... well, I'm so very grateful."

She placed her head on my chest as I pulled her into a hug. "You have no idea what it means to me. This place is my entire world. I had no idea what that really meant until the thought of losing it came so close to being a reality. I owe you everything, John." She looked up, tears glistening in her beautiful blue eyes.

"Nora, I would do anything for you. In case you haven't figured it out yet, I am totally, completely, head-over-heels in love with you. I want to stay here, on this island... with you... forever. I want to spend the rest of my life growing the inn with you. You are IT for me."

Nora's eyes grew wide in surprise. "Would you say that again, please?" she asked.

I touched a hand gently to her face, bringing my lips a breath away from hers. "I love you, Nora."

As I pressed my lips to hers, our bodies melted into one another. The moon shone down on us as the waves rolled over our feet.

"I love you, too, John," she whispered when we finally parted. "I would love nothing more than to have you here, with me, and to grow a beautiful life together."

Without a second thought, I dropped to my knee. "Nora, marry me. Please let me spend the rest of my life here, with you, growing this inn. Growing a family. Growing our love."

A huge smile spread over her beautiful face, and she dropped to her knees as well. "Yes, John. You are every prayer I've ever prayed, every wish I've ever made. You are my person. I love you."

In the moonlight, we could hear the cheers of our friends and neighbors coming from the direction of the deck, but all I could see was Nora.

*Epilogue*

♥

## Nora - Present

I SMILED OUT OVER the railing, watching several young guests run up and down the beach with their parents.

I couldn't believe how blessed my life had been to this point.

It had been over thirty five years since Hurricane Louisa had brought my husband to me. And in those years, we had built more together than I had ever dreamed possible.

The original Heartsail Inn had changed so much over the decades. Beyond the original inn - which was now our personal family residence - and the golf course, we had expanded into a full-service, family friendly resort. The Heartsail Island Resort and Spa now included a 150-room hotel, a premium spa, twenty additional private beach cabins, a full-function marina that included boat and kayak rentals and sight seeing tours, multiple restaurants, tennis courts, walking and bike trails, and a brand new Kid's Club.

The resort had officially put Heartsail Island on the map as a premium vacation destination. And it was all because John had made that fateful trip across the ocean in his little aluminum boat the day after a hurricane.

I smiled and sipped my wine as I heard the door open, revealing a bit of a ruckus inside, and then close again behind me. Without needing to turn, I felt John approach from behind. He slipped his arms around my waist, and I leaned back into his strong, fit body.

"Happy anniversary, my beautiful bride," he whispered into my ear. I loved how he said that to me every time he saw me on the day of our anniversary. It had been like this since the very beginning. Our love, though it developed quickly when we were young, had grown with every day we had spent together.

I turned into his arms and placed my lips lightly against his. "Happy anniversary, love of my life," I replied. "It sounds like it is getting a bit heated in there."

John chuckled. "Yeah, Felicity's got her notebook," he said, a smile coming to his lips.

Our kids, Thomas and Felicity, were throwing us an anniversary dinner that was set to start soon. Felicity, our youngest, was an obsessive planner. Any time we had a get together, she would make all kinds of notes and schedules in her trusty notebook, and drive everyone around her crazy.

I laughed, knowing that the announcement we planned to make during dinner would come as a huge surprise to her.

"We're doing the right thing with her, right, John?" I cuddled my head into the crook of his neck as we turned and looked at the beach.

"She's ready, Nora. Announcing our retirement from the day-to-day running of the resort and naming her General Manager is the right thing. For her and for us. We deserve to step back and enjoy everything that we've built here, and SHE deserves the chance to shine. She's been taking on more and more responsibility over the last few years, and she's going to do a great job as GM."

John rubbed a hand up and down my arm. Even after thirty five years, I still got tingles every time he touched me like that.

"Hey, lovebirds, is it safe to come out here?" Jeremy asked as he and Beth came through the door. Beth was carrying their brand new grandson, Noah, in her arms. Not long after the inn reopened, Jeremy started dating Beth, then had almost immediately moved here to teach at the island's middle school. Now, he was the principal of the school, and every student and parent on the island loved him as much as we did.

Beth handed over the sleeping baby when I stuck out my hands and wiggled my fingers at him. Immediately, I sniffed his fuzzy little head. "I can't wait until Ciara has the baby, and I get one of these little nuggets of my own," I said, nuzzling Noah's little cheek with my nose. Our son, Thomas, and his wife had just announced their pregnancy a few weeks ago, and in a few short months, I would also be a grandmother.

"Soon, mom," Thomas laughed. He ran a hand over Ciara's still-flat belly as they stepped out onto the deck. Felicity followed them, along with Jeremy and Beth's kids, Beau and Stella, and their son-in-law, Marcus.

"Ok, y'all, let's sit. The caterer is about ready to serve," Felicity said. We all made our way over to the beautifully decorated table. As John pulled out my chair for me, he kissed me softly on the cheek and whispered in my ear. "Thank you, my love, for giving me everything I could have ever dreamed of and more. I am so glad Hurricane Louisa destroyed your deck all those years ago."

*THE END*

## Acknowledgments

♥

I never could have written this book without the help of the live writing sessions with my friends at Unchained Writer. Your virtual support, constant encouragement, and steadfast dedication to your craft kept me motivated and engaged throughout this journey. I appreciate all of you, and I look forward to writing many more books alongside you all in the future. Virtual High Five!

And to C and Tea... you are my why. I try every day to show you that anything is possible if you just believe in yourself. Thank you for always being my cheering squad, and for putting up with me when I get a little cranky. I love you both more than you will ever know.

## About the Author

♥

Jenny Fawn loves her kids and pets, warm summer days, copious amounts of coffee, and happily ever after love stories. Her feet hate being in shoes, and she would much rather curl up in a pair of fuzzy pajamas with a good book than get dressed up and go out on the town. When she isn't writing or reading, she can be found floating in her pool (summer), hiding from the cold (winter), or driving her kids to their never-ending list of activities (always!!) in her Western Pennsylvania hometown.

Jenny writes sweet "kissing books" with a whole lot of heart, and just a *hint* of heat. All of her series romances can be read as standalone novels (but it is fun to read them in order!). Like her coffee, she prefers her books light and sweet, and you are ALWAYS guaranteed a happily ever after at the end of every book. (Because NO ONE likes a cliffhanger!!)

Jenny's books are considered "sweet" (PG/PG-13) romances, so you'll never find "colorful" or explicit language, and there are no graphic or gratuitous scenes. (In other words, kissing and touching yes, sex and swearing no!) Because of this, Jenny's books are perfect for most readers - from older teens to great grandmas - who have a romantic soul and love LOVE! (Think: Hallmark movies but on the page instead of the screen!)

Find a complete list of Jenny Fawn's books, join her mailing list, and find out how to get a FREE novella at her website, JennyFawnBooks.com

www.ingramcontent.com/pod-product-compliance
Lightning Source LLC
Chambersburg PA
CBHW030457130626
46549CB00007B/2756

*9 7 9 8 9 8 5 8 9 4 5 0 9 *